HOT & STEAMY STORIES
For Your Own Personal Pleasure

Hot & Steamy Stories:
For Your Own Personal Pleasure

First edition, August 2, 2020, published by Claire Divino
https://clairedivino.substack.com/
https://medium.com/@ClaireDivino

Author: Claire Divino
Cover photo: Alexandr Ivanov

HOT & STEAMY STORIES

For Your Own Personal Pleasure

Claire Divino

TABLE OF CONTENTS

I Wanted Him Inside Me

I'd been secretly watching him for quite a while. I even googled him, I didn't exactly stalk him, but I did check out his pictures. And whenever I did, I couldn't stop staring at his eyes. It gave me the familiar itch between my legs and my imagination went wild. The things I wanted to do with him... oh...

It's better to stare at a picture than to stare at someone in person; that would be embarrassing and the last thing I wanted was to embarrass myself in front of him. So I tried to be subtle when he was around, but that proved to be hard. Just one look into his eyes made me wanna jump him right there and then.

My face flushed and I had to look away. That wasn't exactly subtle but I had no power over it. My body wanted and demanded him. My pussy screamed for his fingers and cock. My lips yearned for his kisses. Not getting any of that, I furiously mounted and rode my dildo, sometimes several times in a row.

While doing it I imagined him between my legs, being as lustful and hard for me as I was lustful and wet for him. It helped me achieve a release but as soon as I saw him again, I was wet and my pussy even more anxious than before.

I asked around whether he had a girlfriend. He didn't but he was recovering from a breakup and I guess that's what made him reluctant to approach me. I wasn't crazy about being a rebound either but I was in lust so I needed to do something. The more I thought about him, the more my pussy itched.

Scared or not, I needed to get more than just temporary relief so I began by not turning my gaze away when our eyes met. I smiled at him. He smiled back and that gave me confidence. I wasn't blushing any longer or at least not that much even though my heart was about to jump out of my chest.

Gosh, he was hot. When I saw him riding his Harley wearing blue jeans and a white t-shirt – fit as he was – I'd need a bucket of ice-cold water poured over me to calm down. I wanted to sit behind him, my arms wrapped around his muscular body, I'd press my body against his, my hand reaching toward the zipper. I'd die to see what was in there.

The chance came sooner than I expected. A group of us decided to have a picnic down at the lake and he offered me a ride. I guess all that smiling and flirting had some effect after all. Off we went, my dream coming true as I sat behind him. Wrapping my hands around his gorgeous body and pressing my boobs against his back was electrifying.

The vibrations of the buzzing engine on the road electrified my clit too. It was as if I were sitting on a giant clit vibrator and my pussy became even hungrier for attention than it already was. I could feel how my nipples became hard and erect and I wondered could he feel them through his t-shirt too.

It seemed that he could, for he said that we were going to take a shortcut. We turned from the main road onto a narrow path and I wondered if this was indeed a shortcut or will it turn out to be a short stop on our way instead. I was praying for the latter since my pussy became too excited for me to be able to handle it much longer.

Whether a shortcut or not, I was determined to make it a short stop. As soon as we lost the sight of traffic on the main road, I did what I've been dreaming of doing all along. I placed my hands on his thighs and then reached for his manhood. Judging by the size and feel, his thoughts were at least as naughty as mine.

I pressed my body tighter against his and started to rub. He stopped the bike at some secluded space and parked it in the shade. He lifted my short dress and started to cares my pussy. I removed my panties and opened his pants.

Seeing his cock made me dripping wet. As his other hand went up and down his impressive shaft, he recognized the urgency of my need, helped me straddle him, and I mounted his cock with abandon.

I put my hands around him and used the rear foot pegs for support as I started to bounce. "Are you always this horny?" he whispered in my ear as I moaned and wriggled on his joystick that brought me even more pleasure than I was hoping for. "Only when somebody is as hot as you are," I responded.

"You are not bad yourself," he said, took off my dress, laid me on the fuel tank, and started to bang me so that I've seen stars. "I wanted to fuck you from the moment I saw you," he continued as his cock went deeper and the sounds of my, by now completely soaked, pussy being fucked hard filled the air.

"I could see in your eyes how much you love cock," he then turned me around, "so I'm gonna give it to you until you beg me to stop." I was now holding the handgrips and he banged me from behind as my clit slid down and up the leather seat as we fucked. It drove me to insanity and I was letting our sounds I never knew I had in me before.

"Tell me how much you love cock," he demanded as he fucked me, his grip on my hips getting more firm, and his violent thrusts getting stronger and faster. "I love cock," I screamed as I came all over his cock and the seat. I could feel how his cock burst with cum inside me while my pussy spasmed in orgasm. "You'll get more on our way back," he promised gently as he held me in his arms.

I'm a Woman and I'm Insatiable

"I have a confession to make. I don't see anything wrong with sex, and lots of it too. I don't fit the traditional stereotype of what a woman should be and how she should behave. You will never have to beg for sex with me because I'm, to begin with, horny. Horny like hell!"

Dr. Tyler listened with a professional, calm look on his face that didn't betray the turmoil he felt inside nor the growing boner in his pants. As a therapist, he'd seen a fair share of sex addicts in his office but never someone like Eve.

She looked like a combination of a movie star and the classiest hooker imaginable. It was as if some icy, platinum blond just stepped out of a Hitchcock's movie and turned into a fair version of Dita von Teese. What was coming out of Eve's mouth was in stark contrast with her polished and impeccable look.

"Watching porn turns me on wildly. It turns me into a wild beast." There was a spark in her eyes, her cheeks blushed, and her bright red lips became even fuller as she continued with growing excitement, "And I like to masturbate, I like to do it a lot."

She paused for a moment, looked at him thoughtfully, and then added, "This is not what is expected of a woman and I know what you're thinking. You'd never expect to hear something like that from someone who looks like me, but to hell with that."

She was right, of course, even though he tried to deny it. Ignoring his feeble attempts, she went on as the temperature and tension in Dr. Tyler's office started to rise along with the uncontrollable hard-on in his pants.

"I want to come clean, I'm tired of pretending, of suppression, of denied passion! The truth is, I'm always ready for something big, and when I say big, I mean BIG. Huge even! I dream big, I need big, I love big — the bigger, the better. Because that's what I've been made for. I mean, I might look petite, but I can take a lot, a whole lot in."

Eve finished her confession, let out a deep sigh, fell back deep into the sofa, and wetted her lips due to all the heat she generated in the room. Her tongue gentle danced across the lips in an ever so sexy way.

This was almost too much for Dr. Tyler who was big. I mean *really* big, huge even, and had always struggled with finding a partner who'd be willing and able to take in something of *that* size. And now here she was, resting on his sofa, telling him how much she craved what he had.

There was nothing he'd love doing more than spreading her legs, pushing his fingers in, and getting her ready for what was to come. He'd unzip his pants (that were just about to explode) and show her what he got for her.

Only, he couldn't do it because she was his patient, they were having a session, and there are rules...

"There is more..." continued Eve blissfully unaware of the predicament he was in, freely sharing her fantasies, "I'm permanently wet and in need of "assistance," and by that I do not mean assistance by just one man. One man won't do, one man simply won't do. There have to be many. Many big men, doing me well, filling me up one after another until I collapse from exhaustion covered in sweat and filled with cum..."

She sighed with a dreamy look in her eyes, staring at some undefined point in the distance, her eyes half-closed, looking sexier than ever. "That's my dream, that's my ultimate wet dream — to be regularly serviced by my own stable of lovers, lovers who are always hard, always willing, always ready, just like me. I'm insatiable."

Dr. Tyler's face gained more than a bit of color.

"And I just love to kiss deep and suck cock," continued Eve with a passion of a true fan. "There's nothing better than sucking dick while being pounded from behind and watching a yet another one getting ready, giving him a hand, making him hard as a rock, knowing that there's more to come, always more."

Dr. Tyler quit smoking years ago but at that moment, he'd give anything for a cigarette. He'd also give anything to fill this teasing bitch to the brim, to spread her legs and enter her with a vengeance, give her insatiable pussy what she craved and more, so much more. This session had turned into a nightmare.

He was about to explode, the hardness in his pants reached the point when he could no longer stand it. He'd either have to jerk off or fuck the horny bitch, and he'd have to do it NOW or he'll soon have cum all over his pants.

At that point Eve looked at him with her big blue eyes and innocent face, looking like a school girl pleading with her teacher to excuse her for being late: "Doctor, please help me, I'm in need of assistance." Dr. Tyler stood up from behind his desk and Eve was finally able to see a giant bulge in his pants.

He said, "I hope you understand that from this moment on you are no longer my client and that I won't be able to ever treat you as my client again. But if you agree, I can treat you in many other ways."

Eve's eyes and mouth opened wide, she spread her legs and nodded in agreement while watching how he unzipped his pants and set his huge boner free. He could see that she wore no panties under her wrap skirt and judging by the looks, her pussy was more than ready and eager to receive him.

She Fitted Him Like a Glove

"You should be a porn star," one of her many lovers said to Belle once. At the time, she was deeply offended by the remark. She never saw herself as someone who should be disrespected simply because of her sex drive.

Even though she was tempted by the idea (just look at how a sex tape turned Kim Kardashian into a star!) she was old enough to understand what happens to most girls once people became aware of their porn career.

The last thing she wanted was to be treated with disrespect. But Belle loved sex and saw no reason to be ashamed of it. If anything, she thought, women like her should be revered, adored, and held in high esteem.

Belle brought pleasure to men, far greatest pleasure than many of these pricks deserved. A *whore*, *bitch*, or *slut* is what some of the idiots whispered into her ear while they fucked her. They were all without exception hard as a rock, they breathed heavily, and they desperately (and often unsuccessfully) tried to not come too soon.

Belle was sexy as hell and the first round in bed was as a rule soon followed by the next. She gave everyone a boner just by walking down the street and knew and loved it too. Some of the men liked to slap her butt during sex. The slaps were never too hard, just enough to make her cheeks blush. She loved a bit of that, a bit of roughness and toughness, she loved manly men.

Her ideal was a man who could arouse her with his strong demeanor, who could make her wet just by looking at her, by letting her know how much she turned him on, what a hard-on she gave him. The man of her dreams would respect her but demand her obedience in bed. He would take her often and wildly and fill her in every sense of the word.

It was hard to find such a man, so Belle kept looking, kept searching, kept kissing frog after frog in the hope of finally finding the prince of her dreams. They came in all shapes and sizes, gave her pleasure beyond measure, they kept her coming over and over again, but she still felt empty inside.

Regardless of how hard they tried, these encounters only left her wanting more, deeper, harder, bigger, wilder. When she had two lovers in a single night, she wished for three, four, ten, more...

After the first left, she couldn't wait for the second one to come, having the next lover at her doorstep less than an hour later. She never needed much foreplay after that, she just wanted it straight in, right there and then. They knew it and loved it...

Belle was now talking dirty into Matt's ear. Only fifteen minutes had passed since Scott left, leaving her hornier than ever. She barely had the time to take a shower and change before Matt came knocking, all excited to see her. She started to bite his ear even before he managed to close the door.

He pressed his masculine body against her so that she could feel his strength and muscles. There was something hard in his pants and she knew exactly what it was. Feeling it made her just as crazy with desire as her ear-teasing drove Matt mad.

'My god, Belle...' was all he could say.

He grabbed her, tore off her skirt, lifted her up, and rubbed his hardness against her crotch. He became even harder upon seeing her tiny panties. He tore those off too while Belle unzipped his jeans and started to play with what she craved more than anything in the world.

He was already as hard as it gets and just the thought of getting it in made her wet.

'Oh, Matt...' Belle's breathing became deeper as she started to suck and play with his gorgeous cock until he couldn't contain himself any longer. His hand reached between her legs to check on her pussy. He could feel how ready she was. Matt was big, but she was so wet that he knew it would only take a couple of strokes to pack it all in.

He lifted her up, lay her on the table, and spread her legs as wide as he could to open her fully. He went in as deep as he could. It took Belle's breath away, for he was so huge she could barely handle it. She bit her lip and moaned due to the mixture of exquisite pain and delight that went through her body like a burning flame.

He fucked her until she started to moan out loud as she began to orgasm. At that point, he couldn't handle it any longer. Belle felt how he came, his magnificent tool pulsating and squirting deep inside her, giving her all that he had. For what seemed an eternity, he kept coming, each squirt accompanied by a low growl and an ever-deeper and harder push until she was finally full.

They both knew this was just the beginning of what was yet to come and she could already feel him getting harder again. Belle turned everyone on and they were all ready for action again almost as soon as they came. Matt was no exception. Taking just one look at the load dripping out of Belle's pussy was enough to make him hard again.

He grabbed her crotch and started to spread the juices all over her silky skin. He fingered her, bringing her to even greater arousal. She was already hungry for more. He took the time to explore just how much of his load was still left in there. First with one finger, then two, and then three.

Belle moaned and begged for more, and then he brought his hand back to her lips. She greedily sucked and licked his fingers like a lollipop. All the way into her mouth he pushed, while her hand reached for his excited cock.

Feeling him getting hard in her skilled hand, she could only whisper, 'Do me, do me again...' Matt was quick to obey. He turned her around, spread the lips of her swollen pussy, grabbed her hips and started to pound.

Belle felt that Matt might be the right one for her. He understood her body better than anyone and knew exactly what to do with it. Finally, for the first time since she could remember, she felt happy and fulfilled by a single man. From then on, there were no more frogs to kiss, there was just Matt.

Work Me, Baby

Liz came to work late but looked so radiant that nobody even thought of reproaching her. Heads turned even more than usual as she glided from the elevator into her office leaving a whisk of seductive perfume in her trace.

Just by the sound of her fast-approaching heels, Aedan, her assistant, knew a macchiato, no sugar, was immediately needed. "And add a bit of Irish Cream if you will, Aedan, please," said Liz with a naughty smile and a wink as she passed his desk.

Aedan blushed, smiled, and winked back. He loved working for Liz, but then who wouldn't. Well, who wouldn't love Liz, to be more precise. Like all other men on the floor, including the gays, Aedan was absolutely smitten with her.

And he knew exactly what a naughty smile, a wink, and "Irish Cream" meant. They were a private joke between them and they meant some extra services Aedan was only too happy to deliver. Liz came up with the code name because he was of Irish descent.

As always after spending the night with one of her many lovers, Liz was burning with desire. Aedan's long, thick club was just what she needed to alleviate some of the unbearable tension she felt between her legs. It would be impossible to work before this was taken care of.

She got rid of her panties in preparation for "a bit of Irish Cream." What Aedan had to offer was hardly a bit, though. It was *a bit much*, rather, at least for most women, but not for Liz. The memory of the first interview she had with Aedan when looking for an assistant brought a smile to her face and made her pussy soaked with the expectation of yet another delicious treat.

Aedan was recommended by one of Liz's friends who knew what Liz was looking for in an assistant besides the administrative skills. A perfect candidate would have to be sexy, fit, well-equipped, open-minded, and ready for action. Just knowing how to work wasn't enough, they would have to know how to work Liz and work her well too.

Aedan turned out to be the perfect candidate. He came to the interview looking like Brad Pitt, wearing a big smile, t-shirt, and blue jeans — an epitome of an American boy which, incidentally, was also the title of the song that was playing on the radio when he stepped into her office.

Liz knew he was it before he even opened his mouth to say hi. They had sex right there and then since that's how Liz tested her candidates to make sure they were "the right fit." And, boy, was Aedan the right fit, the dream fit even! He was a young stud who just landed a dream job — for him, it was like winning a lottery.

Liz was a stunner and he couldn't imagine a guy not being turned on by her. He sure was as soon as he entered her office and closed the soundproof door behind him. To begin with, there was a scent of her irresistible perfume. Liz loved to wear perfumes that were just as deep and sensual as she was.

And then there was her breath-taking cleavage. When he first saw those melons, Aedan could hardly restrain himself from squeezing them. Holding back became impossible when she told him to sit, leaned over him, and brought them closer to his face. He grabbed them with both hands and started to suck her nipples.

There was this special look in Liz's eyes when she was turned on. One could see in them just how much she loved, craved, and adored cock. All it took was one look and Aedan instantly knew what he needed to do next. He unzipped his pants while she lifted her dress and took off her sexy lace panties.

He pulled her toward his towering cock, and Liz started to ride it like a rodeo. She threw her long full hair back and rode as if her life depended on it until she came violently. With his thick, hard cock still inside, he lifted her up and laid her on the sofa.

Gently rocking his tool inside her, he let her rest for a minute and then started to pound harder and harder while lifting her legs up to his shoulders. With each stroke, he got deeper and deeper until he managed to force himself all the way in.

Aedan's pelvis pressed hard on Liz's clit making her wild, and she could feel how his, by now like steel hard, cock reached her cervix and was about to explode into a firework of cum. They both came and Liz screamed with pleasure as Aedan's cock all but ripped her apart in the final assault.

A motherload of white "Irish Cream" flew out of Liz's pussy and she needed a few minutes to catch her breath. When she finally did, all she could say was: "You're hired."

Please, Fuck Me

"Fuck me," Gina whispered while nibbling on Sam's earlobe. He wasn't in the mood, not to mention that it wouldn't be right, but the sound of her voice and warm breath on his neck, let alone the earlobe thing, woke up his penis. He could feel how it began to rise and started to fill the fabric of his jeans.

Gina noticed it too. Her hand reached down from behind and masterfully rubbed the growing boner. He grabbed her hand and unconvincingly tried to push it aside. "Please, fuck me," she whispered softly, licked his ear, and unzipped his pants before he could stop her.

"Gina..." Sam weakly tried to protest as she reached under his underwear and removed all the barriers between his naked hardness and her soft hand. If there was one thing Gina knew, it was how to give a handjob. Gosh, how good that felt. It gave Sam shivers and crushed his will to fight against it.

"Gina, you are such a..." Sam couldn't finish the sentence since Gina now kneeled in front of him and took him in her mouth. "Aaaaaa..." was all he could say watching her lick and suck his cock. And her face, oh my, she was clearly enjoying it and she knew exactly where his weak spots were.

Her hands now traveled under his t-shirt and squeezed his nipples. "Jesus, Gina! Now you are going to get it, I'm going to punish you for this so hard that you'll see stars!" He couldn't contain himself any longer. He lifted her up and placed her on the bed while she skillfully removed the bottom of her bikini.

She spread her legs and showed him her shaved, tiny, barely legal pussy. She touched her lower lips and pulled them apart so that he could see her swollen opening inviting him to enter and rip her apart. "Fuck me," she whispered again.

Even though he knew he really, really shouldn't (her mother would kill him if she knew), he touched her and felt how wet and ready she was. Gina grabbed his hand, pushed his finger in, and repeated, "Please, fuck me!" Sam felt as if her horny little pussy was speaking through her young, innocent mouth.

The air was filled with the scent of coconut oil mixed with sea salt and Gina's juices. All that combined with the sight of her legs spread wide open showing him her pink rose had the effect of an aphrodisiac on Sam. There was no way he could stop now.

He placed the head of his giant, throbbing cock at the entrance and circled around to lubricate it with her wetness. Gina whimpered and gave a little cry as he pushed in while pressing her clit with his thumb.

He was big and she was tight so he progressed slowly and stretched her with short but firm strokes.

"Does it hurt?" he asked to make sure she was fine. Her face was a grimace of pain but her moans spoke of pleasure. "Yes, but it hurts so good," she whispered and added, "Don't stop, please don't stop." He obeyed and pushed deeper and stronger while massaging her clit to keep her juices flowing.

He had to close his eyes not to come at the sight of her body shivering in ecstasy under him, his cock filling her small pussy, her nipples hard like two nails could be seen through the tiny top her white bikini.

"I'm gonna punish you for this, I'm gonna punish you for what you've done to me today," he said and closed his eyes so that he wouldn't come too soon. "You want to be punished little girl, don't you?" he asked as he kept forcing his cock deeper and deeper into the small opening.

Gina was left breathless as he stretched her pussy to the full. She was barely able to breath out a weak "Yes" in response. He grabbed her hips and pulled her body even closer so that they were now completely merged into one. Gina moaned loudly as Sam asked, "Have you ever been pounded hard, little girl, like really, really hard? Because that's what I'm gonna do to you now."

He set her bikini bra-free and watched her bare breasts move with the increasingly faster rhythm he imposed on her pussy. Gina arched her head back, her mouth open with ecstasy. "This is what you get for being a bad girl," Sam whispered in her ear as he pushed deeper and deeper.

"I'm going to fill you up now because that's what bad girls deserve," he said as he pounded her harder and harder. She was just about to explode in orgasm as he stopped, took his cock out, and turned her around. "I'm not going to let you come just yet, as you've been such as a bad, bad girl."

He slapped her bottom, entered her from behind, and kept slapping while he fucked her mercilessly. "Bad girl," he said with each slap followed by yet another deep thrust. Gina has never felt anything so huge enter her from behind. She came loudly with every slap and flooded Sam's cock.

Feeling her squirts Sam couldn't hold it back any longer. He too erupted in one long orgasm. He kept filling her up, squirt after squirt, until they both collapsed with exhaustion. Sam gave her one last slap on the butt and asked, "So, can we continue working on your assignment now?"

How I Slept with Two Lovers in One Day

The memory of this still makes me dripping wet every time I think of it. I had a boyfriend at the time, but our sex life was abysmal, meaning non-existent. After months of this dry season, I couldn't take it any longer and was just about to burst from horniness.

There is only so much masturbation one can do and a dildo is definitely NOT a decent substitute for having a man of flesh and blood doing you the way you need to be done. Nothing can replace entangled bodies, deep kisses, hands traveling across your skin, exploring all of the hidden and less hidden parts.

And so, I ended up getting myself a lover. I started flirting with one of my boyfriend's acquaintances, dragged him to bed, and let him fuck my brains out. Given that my boyfriend did nothing to satisfy me in bed and that he kept rejecting my advances, I felt no guilt whatsoever.

I didn't plan on adding any more lovers to the one I had, but it seems that as soon as a woman gets what she needs, she starts to become extra alluring to every man who passes her by on the street.

And so it happened that I ran into one of my ex-boyfriends who lived, as luck would have it, just around the corner. He invited me over for a cup of coffee and a spliff. Wow, how could I say no to that!

It was a beautiful summer day, I felt better than ever, I was about to meet my new lover later in the day, and I was very much looking forward to some sexual healing I knew he'd provide.

Having a smoke and catching up with my ex-boyfriend sounded like a perfect prelude to a hot date ahead. Call me naive, but I swear I had no idea what my ex-boyfriend had in mind apart from the spliff and coffee.

The stuff he had was strong and it hit me pretty bad. So, when he suggested that we lie down for a while that sounded like a great idea to me. I had no clue that while the joint made me sleepy, it made him horny like hell and as hard as a rock.

So there we were, lying next to each other and before I knew it, his hands were all over my breasts and pussy, while I could feel his enormous hard-on rubbing against me.

I knew I should tell him to stop, but I guess my body language was giving him mixed signals. I had only a light summer dress on and my panties weren't much of a barrier either. Before I knew it, he was fingering me with all his might.

Given the unexpected turn of events, my pussy became as tight as it gets. This, apparently, made him completely lose control. He jumped me from behind and thrust his unbelievably hard penis inside me. It took my breath away.

I still could have stopped it if I really wanted to. But after such a long dry spell, after my boyfriend's attitude made me feel so undesirable, feeling somebody so hard and turned on inside my pussy turned me on too.

I've never felt a cock so hard, so excited to pound me, so determined to fuck me senseless. It was a kind of acknowledgment that I was desirable after all, it was the sexual healing I so badly needed at that time of my life.

I finally felt sexy again, and in the end, we both came and then did it one more time. He knew just how to kiss me deeply, how to play with my tongue, how to finger me to the point just prior to reaching orgasm only to replace the fingers with his extra-long cock, and rip me apart into sheer ecstasy.

We fucked like maniacs and with the windows open the whole street could hear us, for he wasn't exactly quiet either. I barely had the time to clean myself and freshen up a bit, as I was already late for my date.

I appeared at my lover's doorstep with rosy cheeks, messy hair, and apologizing profusely for being late. He didn't care one bit about that. The way I looked probably only made him even hornier, for he pulled me inside and there we went again.

His cock was inside me before I could finish the sentence. The bedroom was right next to the entrance, and before I knew it, I was on all fours on the bed, my dress lifted, panties ripped off, and his cock banging me from behind. He held my hips tight and fucked me as if this was the last day of our lives.

I have to admit I was still so turned on and wet from the previous session that none of this was too much or too soon. I've never been so turned on in my life. I stopped counting how many times I came that day as the whole day felt like one giant ongoing orgasm.

I ended up sucking cock, having every hole filled, swallowing the load and greedily licking the remains of it, and being fucked, fingered, and dildoed to the point of collapse and utter exhaustion.

And I don't regret one moment of it. If anything, I wish for more days like that glorious summer day.

Getting Her Ready for an Orgy

Paul could afford to do just about anything he wanted to. He was one of the privileged 1% and if anything, money was not a problem. The problem was that he fell for a girl half his age and was totally smitten by her.

Normally, that too wouldn't be a problem since Paul was a charmer and could quite easily found his way into any woman's heart. That, in addition to his infinite funds, was usually enough to bring most women to their knees.

He got used to women willingly giving him their hearts to do with as he pleased. But not Viv. Viv was something else. She was a heart-stopping beauty with a perfect body and a kind of personality that turned men into her slaves.

He first saw her when she stepped out of the modeling agency he happened to own and literally stopped the traffic. Bam, bam, bam went Paul's heart at the pace much higher than normal. His jaw literally dropped. The wind played with her long curls and pressed her dress against her gorgeous body. He gasped for air.

Viv was a new swimwear and lingerie model at the agency and she became a star as soon as she appeared on the scene. Unlike runaway models who tend to be rather flat, Viv had some eye-catching curves. Paul instantly knew he must have her.

He ran across the street, introduced himself, and invited her for lunch. Viv accepted and that's how it all started. She was funny and amusing and from that moment on, none other but Viv existed for Paul. He finally found his match. For the first time in his life, he was the one on his knees.

For some reason she grew to like him. But she was also quick to warn him that he won't be able to keep up with her. When they were sipping the second glass of champaign, she nonchalantly told him she had an extremely high sex drive.

"I guess most people would say I'm a nymphomaniac," she laughed as if telling a joke. She took another sip of champagne and looked at him under her brows. "How about you?"

Paul wasn't used to women discussing their sexual habits quite as openly on the very first date, let alone with the owner of a company they worked for. Cleary, Viv was a wild one and she sure didn't waste any time. He liked that, he liked that a lot.

"Well, I sure love sex and I don't shy away from it," he said in response, turning on all his charm. He felt something between his legs. It was Viv's foot testing the waters. He spread his legs a bit more to make it easier for her to rub his excited cock and added meaningfully, "Nor do I shy away from those who love sex."

"Prove it," Viv nonchalantly threw down the gauntlet. They were dining in Ritz, which is where he was always staying when in Paris so he took her by the hand and led her to his penthouse suite without even trying to hide the boner. Viv jumped him as soon as they entered the room.

He grabbed her booty and rubbed her pussy against his hard cock. She gave a little cry. Both her full lips and the lips of her pussy were swollen with desire. He touched her down there to feel the throbbing of her tortured pussy that was in urgent need of fulfillment and satisfaction.

He pushed his fingers in so that burning hot walls parted while Viv stroked his eager cock as they stumbled towards the bed. She pushed him on the bed, straddled him, and slowly mounted herself.

Fully impaled on his cock, Viv started to ride. The way she rode him, naked with her long hair loose, reminded Paul of wild horses. She was wild and beautiful, loud and shame-free, wonderfully tight and horny, an embodiment of sexuality with a libido of a young stag.

Just from watching her full breasts move with the rhythm of her forceful thrusts Paul almost came. She was pure perfection and as such perfect for the orgies of the secret society, Paul was a member of.

Only the best would do for that group and Viv was the best of the best.

"Do you have plans for the weekend?" Paul asked after he loaded her with his seed. She was laying in his arms playing with what he put inside her and licking her fingers to check the taste. She was already ready for more.

"Whatever plans I have, they can be altered if what you have in mind would be more satisfying," Viv playfully teased in response. "Oh, I can assure you, what I have in mind will be far more satisfying than anything else you could think of," Paul said as he grabbed her breasts and started to kiss and gently bite her hardened nipples.

He adored them, the boobs, he could hold them in his arms and play with them forever. These boobs were, just like Viv, made for fucking and sucking.

He was sure other members of the society will feel the same way too. He was also sure that Viv will, for once, be satisfied, truly satisfied after they are done with her. There will be no end of men and they will do her in every conceivable way.

She will get filled with cock after cock and they won't stop until she won't be able to take it any longer. He was getting hard again just from thinking about it, seeing in his mind how they bang her, how her pussy takes their cocks in while all those who are waiting on their turn masturbate around her.

She'll wear nothing but high heels and a feathered mask and her fully exposed pussy will be theirs for the night. This turned him on and his cock bounced up all hard and ready again. He got on top of her and entered.

God, how tight she was, stretching her while seeing her face and hearing her cries and moans was almost too much to bear. His cock was twitching with excitement.

He went faster and faster. He fucked her hard until she cried in ecstasy. He spread her legs wider while watching her gorgeous dancing boobs, placed his hands under her knees to lock them in place, and hammered her as hard as he could.

He squashed her clit with every thrust so that she started crying out in pain and pleasure. As his throbbing cock filled her up with another load, Viv loudly exploded in a squirting orgasm too.

"I want more," was the first thing Viv said after they came back to their senses. "You'll get more," promised Phil, "You'll get a lot more than that. Just wait for the weekend."

The Steamiest Ride Ever

It was a hot summer day and my ex and I decided to drive to the seaside. We were both single (again!) and having all the time on our hands, the suggestion to go for a drive and take a plunge in the sea was just what I needed.

Oh, summer! The hotness wasn't just in the air but in our bodies as well. I wore a tight bodysuit with low cleavage nicely filled with my large boobs, and shorts. Given that we were going for a swim, I thought it would be practical to wear something that could be easily removed.

I wasn't thinking about having sex; having a swim was what I desired most due to the heat. But upon seeing me the thought, apparently, crossed my ex's mind and wouldn't leave it alone. I didn't notice it since I wasn't paying attention to his pants. If I were, I'd most certainly have seen a growing boner in there.

I was just sitting next to him, listening to the music, wind in my hair, appreciating the scenery, enjoying an unexpected joyride, and looking forward to that plunge. In the meantime, as it seemed, my ex enjoyed the scenery of my boobs and had another kind of plunge in mind — a deep dive into my pussy.

All of sudden and with no warning he took a turn to the side road, turned off the engine, and before I knew it, I felt his hand between my legs while the other one embraced me. He kissed me on the mouth and started to play with my clit.

His skilled fingers were soon inside me, making me wet, for he knew my body inside and out. As surprising as this turn of events was, his fingers played me so well and made me so horny that I couldn't resist enjoying this unexpected bonus to our trip. I set his boner free and he removed my shorts with a single pull.

Apparently, I was doing my part of undressing him too slowly for his taste, for he lost his patience before I could even start giving him a handjob and he was on top of me the very next second.

All I could do was spread my legs and prepare for the welcome assault. He grabbed his cock, placed it at the entrance of my pussy and started to bang me like a maniac.

He growled and groaned as he mercilessly pounded me closer and closer to orgasm. He fucked as if he didn't have pussy for ages and needed it more than anything in the world. Seeing him so aroused, that almost frantic look in his eyes, turned me on beyond belief.

I became so wet that you could hear the sound of my soaked pussy as he rammed it and it made us both even wilder. He greedily grabbed my boobs and then buried his head in them and sucked them as I came.

My body shivered as the walls of my pussy went through a series of spasms that squeezed his cock so that it too burst in a giant load of cum too.

As we lay there catching our breath, I could feel him already getting hard inside me again. I placed my hand on his perineum and started to gently rub it while playing around the entrance of his butt.

In response, he started to drill me again, getting harder with each thrust. I knew this was going to be one long ride and that we'd both need that plunge once we finally reached the sea.

He Entered Me from Behind In a Room Full of People

I woke up due to a finger entering my pussy. We were on a weekend getaway, a group of us rented a cottage and some of us had to sleep on the floor in the attic since there weren't enough bedrooms to accommodate us all. It was like camping, only inside the house.

A cute, tall guy was sleeping next to me and at the crack of dawn, he tested the waters of my pussy by gently pushing his finger inside. My pussy is highly excitable and it instantly got wet. I liked how this guy looked and how bold he was to dare to touch me like that.

We flirted the night before and even though nothing happened during the night since I retired earlier, he must have woken up with a hard-on. My pussy enthusiastically responded to his fingering. He pulled my panties down and I could feel that he had already removed his too.

He was big, one of the biggest cocks I ever had inside me. Feeling his giant boner on my back fired me up and I couldn't wait to get it inside. There were people lying all around us, though. Everyone was still asleep, so we couldn't get loud and needed to be discreet.

I couldn't imagine staying quiet once that giant beast would enter me. I knew it would stretch me far beyond what I was used to and I knew it would make me moan if not scream with pleasure. He anticipated that too and after making me dripping wet with his fingers, he placed his hand over my mouth and slowly entered me from behind.

OMG was all I could think as his huge shaft electrified every single nerve-ending in the walls of my pussy. I wanted him to start banging me so badly, I wanted to ride and bounce on his cock like a maniac but instead, we had to do it slowly and there was no chance of loud ramming I love and need so much.

He managed to pack his whole cock in, which took some time and was, given his enormous size, an achievement in itself, and then we just lay there. I was coming just from having him inside and he was trying not to come. We were both turned on wildly and even more so due to the presence of others.

My orgasming pussy pulsated and massaged his cock, I thought I was going to burst since I wanted to move my hips and dance on his cock so much but had to stay still instead. He held my breasts and played with my nipples under the cover as his cock twitched inside me with excitement.

The tension kept building up, not just from having him inside me but even more so from having to hold back and not being able to fuck each other crazy like we desperately wanted to. It drove us both mad as we'd never before been so turned on and horny but unable to get a release.

We lay there like that until eventually everyone else got up and left, at which point, he could finally properly fuck me. He came all over my butt after just a few strokes. Everyone could still hear us, so we needed to do this as quietly as possible and it didn't in the least quench our insatiable lust.

We took the first chance to get away and found a secluded place in the woods where we could get loud and fuck to our heart's desire. He lay me down on the soft moss, I spread my legs and used my hands to open my smoking hot and dripping pussy for him. Seeing his giant hard cock both scared and turned me on at the same time.

I couldn't believe I had something of that size inside me. As he mounted me, I watched in disbelief and my jaw dropped as his enormous shaft disappeared into me, first one-third of it, then one half, then three quarters and then the whole of it at which point I came and didn't stop coming.

I screamed, squealed, and moaned as he rammed me, the sheer size of it was enough for me to keep orgasming as he filled me up and I could feel him hit the entrance of my womb with every stroke. I still find it unbelievable that I was able to handle that monster and he was ecstatic since he could get it all the way in, which was something he was never able to do with other girls.

This turned him on so much that he wanted to fuck me one more time even though he already came twice and I stopped counting my orgasms. He turned me around and started banging me again even though his cock was only semi-erect at that point. He was so huge, though, that he turned me on at even half the size.

I could feel a giant load of cum flowing down my thighs as he pounded me from behind. My sighs and moans as well as the sight of his cum dripping from my pussy made him hard like a rock again and I was deeply impressed by his unbelievable stamina.

Our bodies were clearly made for each other and this time we reached the climax in unison and both came in a loud crescendo that still makes me wet every time I think of it.

The Surprise Birthday Party

Jack loved Natalie with all his heart and would do anything to make her happy. She was the cutest and sexiest girl you can imagine and she became absolutely wild when turned on. Jack could hardly keep up with her and knew he'd sooner or later need reinforcement.

He was also familiar with Natalie's sexual fantasies, the favorite of which was being tied in bed and fucked by a group of gorgeous looking men whom she imagined would take turns and do all sorts of things to her. He decided to make her wish true for her birthday.

Finding gorgeous looking men wasn't a problem since Jack was influential in the film industry and personally knew even the biggest stars. He also knew that quite of few of them wouldn't in the least mind sticking their dicks inside Natalie. Her charming naivete combined with sex appeal was irresistible.

That also went for her perfect body and long, slim legs, which she loved to show off. Natalie sure knew how to turn heads. All he had to do now was pick the hottest guys and stage the scene for her 25th birthday. It will be the greatest surprise party ever!

Natalie didn't have a clue about what was waiting for her in the bedroom when she got home after spending an afternoon celebrating with her girlfriends. For all she knew, Jack and she would be alone and spend the evening making out and having a whole lot of sex.

She was already wet with anticipation when she walked in wearing one of her sexiest slit dresses. The slit went so high up her thigh that Jack easily slipped his hand in to feel her soaked panties. He teased her pussy through the panties to fire her up and prepare her for the party.

He offered her a glass of nicely cooled champaign and put a blindfold over her eyes while she sipped it. "I have a surprise for you," he whispered in her ear, "and I think you'll like it." Natalie's heart started to beat faster, "What is it?" she asked all excited, but he wouldn't tell.

"You'll see," he took her by the hand and led her into the bedroom where the guests already waited for her. Everybody got hard at the sight of Natalie's gorgeous boobs and hard nipples that could be clearly seen through the fabric of her spaghetti-strapped silk gown.

As she walked in, the slit on her dress opened to reveal her lean leg in sexy stilettoes. Jack grabbed her from behind, his hands slowly traveling up her body. He took some time to caress her breasts and pressed his hard-on against her booty.

The men in the room watched and Natalie could hear them unzip and drop their pants. This, in addition to feeling Jack's hands all over her body and his wanting penis rubbing against her butt turned her on like never before. The fact that she couldn't see made the scene even more intense.

Only now she became aware of sensual music playing in the background and she and Jack started to move in the rhythm as he lifted her dress and released his cock. He rubbed it between her thighs. One of the men now approached and started to caress Natalie's boobs.

His scent was enchantingly erotic, and Natalie couldn't stop herself from offering herself to him. The man started to kiss her neck and she could feel his unshaven face on her skin and felt his fingers rubbing her clit. She instantly came when Jack entered her from behind while the man worked her clit.

They kissed and she sucked the man's tongue as if it were a cock. He understood what she wanted and before she knew it, she was on all four, Jack banging her from behind and the man sticking his glorious boner into her mouth.

Natalie's sighs and moans became louder as she sucked and got fucked at the same time, and the two men groaned with pleasure. She still had a blindfold on but she could hear the sound of rubbing cocks all around them. She knew she will get a lot more cock before the end of the party.

Anticipation aroused her even more and she came yet again as Jack's pounding reached a crescendo and both men shoot their loads deep inside her. By now she was dripping wet, full of cum mixed with her own juices but this only made her hornier. She wanted more and she wanted it now.

Natalie could feel several hands lifting her up and carrying her towards the bed. Along the way, somebody set her dress loose and she was now lying naked on the bed, her hands tied to the bed, her legs spread apart, cum dripping from her pussy, ready to be entered again.

She could feel hands on her body, fingers pushed inside her mouth so that she sucked them hungrily, her breasts and nipples licked, sucked, and grabbed, and somebody's anxious cock was already at the door of her wet, pulsating pussy. She's never felt so helpless and at the same time so unbelievably horny.

"Give it to me," she begged and lifted her hips to offer her pussy to the huge cock who teased but wouldn't yet enter. The man, as if only waiting for her command, grabbed her hips, thrust it in and started to bang her so that the sound of clasping flesh and juices filled the room.

Natalie threw her head back, lips opened in ecstasy, and got another hard and needy cock pushed inside her mouth while two more landed in her hands. She came violently when the man who fucked her filled her up while she was giving the handjobs, his penis twitching and throbbing deep inside her, his pelvis grinding her clit.

As soon as he was done, one of the men placed himself underneath her and started to fuck her from below, while another one entered from above. She now had two penises inside her vagina, stretching her well-lubricated pussy to the limit while she devotedly sucked a yet another one in her mouth as the man fiercely rubbed it.

By now Natalie stopped counting the orgasms, it all turned into one giant, on-going orgasm. As she sucked the last drop of cum from the cock that just exploded into her mouth, she could hear how the two men who fucked her in unison exhaled loudly and felt how their throbbing cocks simultaneously shot inside her too.

She lay there enjoying the last waves of the longest orgasm, a river of cum flowing from her pussy, exhausted, happy, and fulfilled in a way she never thought would be possible before. Jack gently removed the ties and blindfold, kissed her on the mouth, and said, "Happy birthday, my love."

She Finally Got What She Craved

The first thing Emma noticed when she approached the stairs leading to the venue was a dashing stranger chatting with a group of people. There was something about him that completely erased everyone else in the picture — all she could see was this man as if the other people around him wouldn't exist.

Not only other people, as it turned out this went for other things as well, such as the stairs. She tripped and was about to fall when the dashing stranger caught her just before she was about to hit the stairs. "Christ!" she exclaimed shocked by the fall as well as the effect he had on her.

"Well, not Christ, but Chris. Close enough, though!" he corrected her and smiled with a smile she won't be able to forget any time soon. His playful blue eyes were another feature she couldn't get out of her mind. She blushed, thanked him, and rushed inside to avoid further embarrassment.

"Focus!" Emma rebuffed herself, "You are not here to fool around, you are here to learn!" She followed the signs and found an empty sit in the front row of the hall where the lecture was about to begin.

It was the first day of the ten-week program for startups and the last thing she needed was to make a fool of herself. She tried to slow down her heartbeat and banish the images of Chris's eyes and messy blond hair from her mind. She almost succeeded when he entered the hall.

"Oh. My. God! He's taking the course as well," Emma blushed again and looked at her feet as if that could help. "OK, so just focus on the lecture, and all will be well," she instructed herself and lifted the gaze only to see him standing at the podium looking straight at her.

Clearly, this won't be as easy as she hoped for. She weakly smiled back and then spent the whole lecture trying to take notes and actually pay attention to what he was saying. It was torture. As he went through with the presentation, she had to look up and check the slides. And whenever she did, she ended up checking him instead.

His butt was to die for and she couldn't stop thinking about what was on the front side of it and how large it might be. If there's any truth to that, the size of his nose and the length of his fingers spoke about a substantial asset. She had to cross her legs to keep the wetness of her pussy somewhat contained.

Afterward, she couldn't wait to get home and ride the largest dildo in her collection with her eyes closed, orgasming while imagining sitting on Chris and being violated by his super-sized cock.

When she came to the next lecture, Chris was standing next to the entrance as if waiting for her. He greeted her and playfully commented how surprised he was that she left so soon after the first event. He expected her to stay and ask questions given how much attention she was paying to him during the lecture.

Emma wished the ground would swallow her. She blushed again (this now seemed to be the *fil rouge* of this whole embarrassing experience) and tried to get inside just as he moved to get in too. The unintentional result was that her perky breasts brushed against his arm.

Since he was wearing a short sleeve t-shirt, this meant he could feel her hardened nipples too. She looked at him not knowing what to say or do and noticed with more than a bit of surprise that she wasn't the only one red in the face. He hurried to the men's room and left her wondering.

She could hear the water splashing from behind the door as if he were trying to cool down or something. Could it be that she turned him on just as much as he turned her on? She felt the blood pumping in her veins. She barely contained herself from following him in the men's room and...

NO, she needed to cool down! She sternly reminded herself that she was here to finish the course and get the certificate and that this was the only thing that mattered. It took Chris quite a while to get back in the lecture hall and when he finally walked in, her resolve vanished in thin air.

It seemed to her that the front of his pants looked somewhat more pronounced than normal. It seemed as if something large was in there and it wasn't hard to guess what that might be. The sight gave Emma wings.

She came to the next lecture wearing a dress with a killer cleavage she knew would be enough to raise the dead let alone kindle the already burning fire. As always, he stood next to the door waiting for her. The look on his face told her everything she needed to know.

"Emma, could you please follow me to my office," he asked when she approached. No words were necessary when he closed the door behind them. They went after each other as two starved beasts, hands unzipping, grabbing, removing the obstacles while lips and tongues danced their frantic dance.

"We only have the time for a quickie," Chris whispered in her ear, "but I want you to stay late tonight so that I can take good care of you." Before she could answer he lifted her up and placed her on his desk. Emma spread her legs wide open.

Chris's boner was huge and he had to put his hand over her mouth to muffle her ecstatic screams when his shaft stretched her. "God, how you turn me on," he said while pounding her.

His words fired her up even more and she orgasmed with every whisper. "I thought my pants were going to burst when you brushed your tits against me," he continued. "I had to go and jerk off but was hard again as soon as I saw you."

Emma could feel how his enormous, pulsating cock squirted inside her, filling her up. When he finished, Chris kissed her and said: "How about coming early before every lecture and leaving late?"

Friends Who Shared Everything

When Adam saw Ellie at the mall, he couldn't believe his eyes — she came back! Finally! Ever since she left for college, Adam couldn't wait to see her again. And now here she was, looking better than ever.

Ellie always reminded Adam of Reese Witherspoon. As a child, Ellie looked like an angel with her blond curly hair, blue eyes, and rosy cheeks. She still looked like an angel, only this time more like Victoria's Secret angel since she was shopping for lingerie in Victoria's Secret store.

Adam called her name and Ellie lifted her eyes from a lace teddy she was holding in her hands. Gosh, Adam would give anything to see her wear that sexy little thing!

"Adam!" she exclaimed and excitedly signaled him to come in. "It's great to see you! I was meaning to call but wanted to treat myself to some new pieces first." Ellie was known for her love of lingerie and her taste was impeccable. She always looked like a princess and that included her underwear.

That was one of the things that always came to mind when he was thinking of her, which was often. Ellie and Adam used to hang out together a lot in high school. Ellie, of course, was one of the most popular girls in school. She could have spent her time with anyone she wanted yet he chose him and his friends.

This still baffled him. Adam, Josh, and Ron were not jocks or football superstars, and they certainly didn't have the most muscular or fit bodies in school. What they had, though, was wit and humor. They were a bit shy but then also loyal and courageous.

They simply adored Ellie and she knew they'd do anything to protect her. She felt safe and loved when she was with them and she knew she could trust them. The last thing she wanted was to get involved with guys who'd brag about having sex with her.

There was none of that with her trio. She lovingly called them her pack of wolves. And now she was back and she gave Adam a kiss on the cheek and asked him how he and the guys were doing. "Well, come and see for yourself," said Adam. The guys, as it turned out, rented a house together and Ellie was more than welcome to visit.

"In fact, why don't you come over right now," Adam added feeling encouraged and bold by how excited she was to see him, not to mention the shopping bags full of Ellie's new lingerie. Maybe, just maybe, there was even a chance of seeing her wear some of that!

The truth was, the three of them were starved for sex. Other than occasional (and anything but satisfying) flings, they had none since she left. They craved her plump pussy, her giggles, her masterful fingers, and, last but not least, her soft lips. If anyone, Ellie knew how to suck and rub one to ecstasy.

Ellie could see a spark in his eyes and knew exactly what he was thinking. She felt a sense of relief — so the guys didn't get hooked up after all. What she feared the most was that they'd all have girlfriends and there would be no more hanky-panky with the three of them.

She smiled and said, "Sure, I'd love to!" He smiled back at her, grabbed her shopping bags, and said, "After you, princess." He loved looking at her swaying hips as she walked in front of him. Her perfect ass was all he could think of.

Josh and Ron were sunbathing in front of the pool at the back of the house when Adam and Ellie arrived. The guy jumped to their feet in surprise.

"Ellie, you're back! You have no idea how much we've missed you!" Before Ellie knew it, she was given a comfy lounge seat and Ron was quick to mix Pina Colada, her favorite summer cocktail. Sipping the drink with her three favorite guys was pure bliss.

The drink made Ellie bold and hot so she didn't object when the kisses on the cheeks turned into deep kisses on the mouth and the hands started to caress her body.

The guys took off her clothes and gasped when they saw sexy lace she wore underneath — it was crotchless so all they needed to do was spread her legs and her pussy was theirs for the taking.

Josh was the first to kneel in front of Ellie, entered her with his fingers, and used his tongue and teeth to gently tease and play with her clit while Ron couldn't get enough of Ellie's glorious perky tits.

He eagerly sucked and played with her nipples while Ron and Josh enjoyed various parts of Ellie's body, Adam brought his boner to her mouth. There was no one in this world who'd give head the way Ellie did and when she took it into her mouth, Adam was instantly transported to heaven.

She knew exactly where all the erogenous zones were located, how to rub, lick, and suck them, and how much pressure to apply. She stroked the base of Adam's cock with her hand and sucked the head while using the tip of her tongue to massage the sensitive spot right under the head.

It turned her on to feel how his excitement and his penis grew. She repeatedly took the cock in all the way down to her throat and then went up again with her full lips tightly pressed around his shaft.

This made her so wet that Josh felt it was high time to fuck her the way she deserved — deep, hard, and well. He mounted her from behind and gave her the treatment she needed. This was exactly what she wanted.

Ellie came loud and Adam couldn't hold back any longer. His cock erupted all over her bust. It was now Ron's turn to offer his cock to her. Ellie eagerly took him in her mouth and did her magic again while Josh pounded her.

Seeing Ellie give head to Ron made Josh explode inside her. Ron was quick to take over and made sure the lady was fully satisfied. "Guys, you have no idea how much I've missed you," said Ellie when she caught her breath. To this, the guys responded as one, "We missed you more!"

Sex Turned Into a Never-Ending Ecstasy

I don't do drugs but I sometimes like to experiment. I always opt for natural substances, though, such as mushrooms and pot, and would never touch anything that comes in a form of pills or dust. It's just not safe.

Pot, though, makes me sleepy rather than horny and while I had sex after smoking a joint, this usually happened only if my lover instigated it and turned me on too. But with this one mushroom trip, we both quite unexpectedly turned into sex maniacs.

We ingested them at his place, taking the time to chew them well to get the most out of them. And then we waited, a bit nervous and excited, for the magic to happen. We didn't expect it to be erotic or sensual. We just expected something weird to happen to our perception.

Instead, lust slowly crept upon us, the kind of I never felt before. It was sensual and overwhelming. We started to kiss and couldn't stop. It was not a hot, fast, quickie kind of lust that demands fast and furious satisfaction. Instead, it was an unending desire to feel and sense and merge our bodies and we felt the need to keep fucking for hours.

I've never seen a man so effortlessly remaining hard even after multiple orgasms. I don't even know how many times he came; all I know is that I kept coming and that we both couldn't get enough of it.

After the shroom kicked in, we started to kiss in the living room where we were listening to music. It was slow but incredibly intense kissing and we were soon all over each other. He grabbed my crotch while I was still fully dressed and I melted in his arms even though he didn't even touch my skin.

Likewise, I could feel him getting hard through his pants without even opening the zipper. Everything was much more intense, there was this sense of deep connection between us and desire that far exceeded the purely physical level of existence.

When we kissed, well before he even entered me, I felt as if we already started to melt into each other. When he slipped his hand inside my panties, caressed my clit, and then pushed his fingers inside me, I felt a sense of bliss incomparable to anything I felt before.

It had a kind of a slow-motion feel to it too, or, better yet, it felt as if time disappeared. I helped his fingers go deeper. Feeling them stroking the walls of my pussy while he pressed his thumb on the clit resulted in waves of sensual pleasure that turned my whole body into a fluid, ecstatic wave.

Our bodies felt like a wave; it was as if we turned into water. I embraced him and let out a series of deep sighs as my body raved on his fingers. I slipped my hand under his shirt and traveled across his skin. My hand went up, reached the nipple and started to squeeze.

In response, his fingers ravaged me even more and he bit my neck. My hand moved down toward his pants. I reached inside and felt the tip of his hard cock there, right below the belt. It was dying to be set free.

I opened the buttons and released the beast. While still firmly mounted on his fingers that did wonders to my pussy, I started to gently stroke his impatient cock. He climbed on top of me and we melted in ecstasy when he entered me.

It was the slowest and most sensual sex I've ever had. He fucked me with slow strokes and I kept coming while we were lost in each other's eyes. We saw each other's rapture in them and we were drowning in it.

Since the sofa became uncomfortable, he lifted me up and carried me to the bedroom still mounted on his erect cock. He lay me on the bed, lifted my legs, and placed them on his elbows. My pussy was completely open to him and he went in as deep as it gets.

The rapture of this deep-dive turned us on even more and he increased the pace but still, there was no sense of urgency, no hurry, no exhaustion just an ecstatic union of two intertwines bodies with no end of pleasure in sight.

I then turned around and lifted my butt with legs apart so that he was able to fuck me from behind and continue with the deep-dive I love so much if the cock isn't too big. His was just the right size and so he entered my pussy and fucked me into yet another series of orgasms.

Time didn't matter as we changed positions, we had no idea how much of it has passed but at one point, I was so full of cum that we decided to take a shower. As we got up, he wasn't as hard as before so I thought that was the end of the already hours-long marathon, but I was wrong.

In the shower, we kissed with eyes closed. Warm water running down our naked bodies felt divine. Before long, I could feel his hand reaching between my legs and something hard rubbing against me. He fingered me again and then turned me towards the wall. I lifted my hands to find support on the shower wall and he entered me from behind.

He held my body tight, his hands grabbed my breasts and I could feel his cock thrusting in me until we both came one last time. The shrooms were losing their grip and we started to feel the exhaustion. Yet, the feeling of rapture, ecstasy, and bliss lingered on long after we went to bed to get some well-deserved sleep.

Fill Me Up

I love it when you enter me, slowly at first and then faster and faster. I love feeling your hardness, with every fiber of my pussy, trembling with pleasure, melting under you, into you. I love it when you suck my breasts while I massage your cock, and you finger me and play with my clit till I come, hips high, followed by a loud sigh of release.

I love it when you tease and gently slap me with your hard shaft and then let me catch it with my mouth. I love watching how it rises higher and higher, feeling how it gets harder and harder in my hand. I love it when you lift my legs and spread my pussy, and look me in the eye with that look so that I know and can hardly wait for what's to come.

I love to feel you deep inside, all the way in, your pelvis grinding my clit hard while the head of your shaft hits the entrance of my womb. I love it when you pound and drill me and the tension builds to the point of unbearable. I love it when we can hardly take it any longer but we somehow manage to keep going. I love to hear you moan and see how my moans turn you on too.

I love wrapping my legs and arms around you, getting as close to you as possible, feeling as much of your skin on mine as I can. I love going through your hair with my hands and I love it when you grab and playfully pull mine. I love your lips on my neck and ears and I love my nails on your back.

I love it when we kiss deeply and our lips and tongues dance and merge in ecstasy. I love massaging and squeezing your cock with my inner muscles while you fuck me, but as heavenly as all this is, nothing can compare to you coming deep inside me and giving me every single drop of your load.

Nothing can compare to your throbbing cock, to that last few thrusts you give me, to how connected we feel when you keep shooting deep inside me, our bodies moving as one, as we press our pelvises together so that they almost merge, and then relaxing in each other's arms, my pussy full of your cum.

Nothing can compare to pleasure and boundless sense of fulfillment I feel when you fill me up, when I feel your silky load deep inside me, when we both come in the synced pulsating rhythm of both my pussy and your cock, when I feel that this kind of bliss is why life might be worth living after all.

About the author

Like the protagonists in her stories, Claire Divino loves good sex and is not afraid of showing and sharing her love with others. Subscribe to Claire's stories and never miss the heat.

https://clairedivino.substack.com/

Read Claire's stories on Medium
https://medium.com/@ClaireDivino